"Hold fast to your dreams, for without them life is a broken winged bird that cannot fly."
—LANGSTON HUGHES

"Every line means something."
—JEAN-MICHEL BASQUIAT

"A person who never made a mistake never tried anything new."
—ALBERT EINSTEIN

"Change will not come if we wait for some other person or some other time. We are the ones we've been waiting for. We are the change that we seek."
—BARACK OBAMA

"Keep us flying!"
—TUSKEGEE AIRMEN

"We came in peace for all mankind."
—NEIL ARMSTRONG

SIMON & SCHUSTER BOOKS FOR YOUNG READERS
An imprint of Simon & Schuster Children's Publishing Division
1230 Avenue of the Americas, New York, New York 10020
Copyright © 2011 by Madstone, Inc. d/b/a Frecklestone
For information about special discounts for bulk purchases, please contact
Simon & Schuster Special Sales at 1-866-506-1949 or business@simonandschuster.com.
The Simon & Schuster Speakers Bureau can bring authors to your live event. For more information or to book an event,
contact the Simon & Schuster Speakers Bureau at 1-866-248-3049 or visit our website at www.simonspeakers.com.
Book design by Laurent Linn
The text for this book is set in Brinar Pro.
The illustrations for this book are rendered in acrylic, gouache, pencil, and collage.
Manufactured in China / 1010 SCP
2 4 6 8 10 9 7 5 3 1
Library of Congress Cataloging-in-Publication Data
Lee, Spike.
Giant steps to change the world / Spike and Tonya Lewis Lee ; illustrated by Sean Qualls. — 1st ed.
p. cm.
Summary: Pursuing one's own path in life takes courage, strength, and perseverance, as demonstrated
by such inspirational leaders as Barack Obama, Albert Einstein, and Muhammad Ali.
ISBN 978-0-689-86815-3
[1. Perseverance (Ethics)—Fiction. 2. Goal (Psychology)—Fiction. 3. Conduct of life—Fiction.]
I. Lee, Tonya Lewis. II. Qualls, Sean, ill. III. Title.
PZ7.L514857Gi 2011
[E]—dc22
2009027622

Giant
Steps
to
Change
the World

For Satchel and Jackson
—S. L.

For Satchel, Jackson, Connor, and Carter—
whose steps are sure to rock the world—
and to Mom, Dad, and all of my ancestors,
thank you for leaving such big,
solid shoes for me to fill!
—T. L. L.

For my sisters, Hope, Faith, and Angela.
And in memory of my mother
and my great-aunt Edith.
—S. Q.

SPIKE LEE & TONYA LEWIS LEE

Giant Steps
to Change the World

Illustrated by SEAN QUALLS

SIMON & SCHUSTER BOOKS FOR YOUNG READERS

NEW YORK   LONDON   TORONTO   SYDNEY

On some days your dreams may seem too far away to realize.

Listen to the whispers of those that came before . . .

those who had hard days but dared to make their dreams come true.

The road won't be easy.

People will try to exclude you,

but you must leap over hurdles—

like the Olympic athlete who won the gold

They made **giant steps** to make the world a better place

and left **big shoes** for you to fill.

the way the freedom fighter encouraged the enslaved to ride the railroad to safety so that all could be free.

You won't always have the answers.

Ask for help and guidance—

like the teacher who started a school for children thought

unteachable and turned them into scholars.

Others may try to force you to ignore your principles. Stand your ground—

like the heavyweight champion who refused to pick up a gun against a fellow human being.

If they tell you, "No, you are not smart enough,"
prove them wrong with your fortitude and brilliance—
like the neurosurgeon with magic hands—because they
were wrong about him and they are wrong about you.

Your heart will ache for your countryman who is hungry. Go to him and feed him—

like the woman who dedicated her life to

feeding the hungry and healing the sick

and asked for nothing in return.

When you witness the ills that poverty and

lack of education heap on a community,

lend your voice—like the poet who wrote

of the pain and the beauty

of neighborhoods forgotten.

The Negro Speaks of Rivers